# Little Bo Peep

## and Her

# BAD, BAD SHEEP

A MOTHER GOOSE **HULLABALOO**

by A.L. Wegwerth
illustrated by Luke Flowers

**CURIOUS FOX**
a capstone company–publishers for children

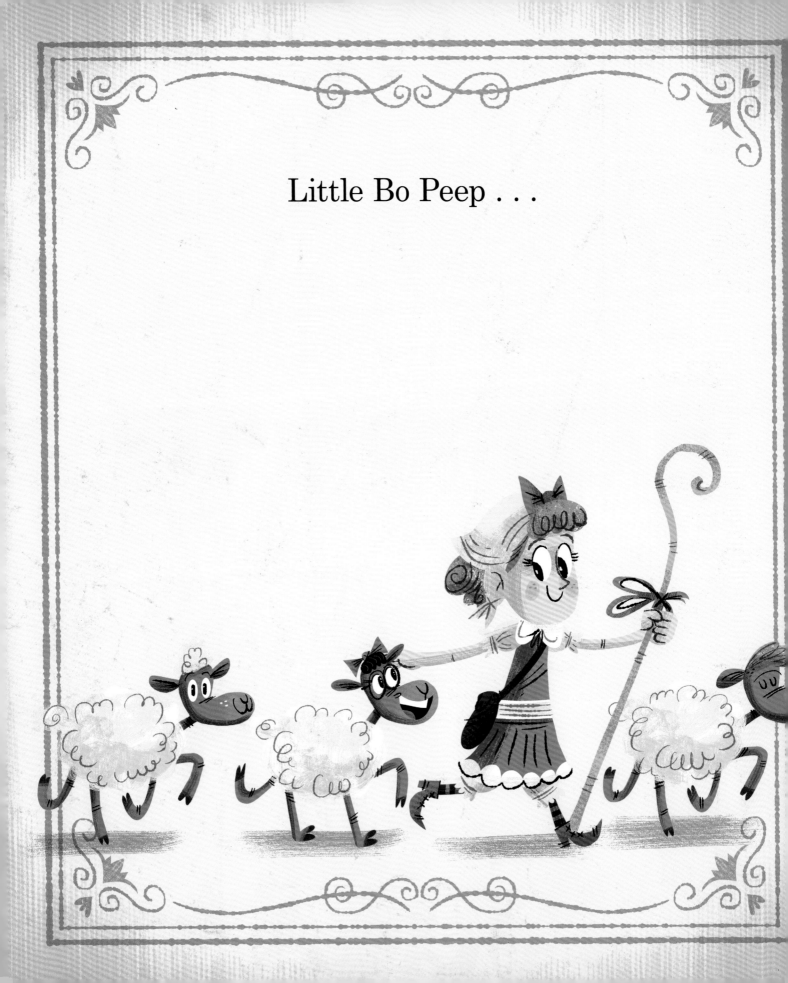

Little Bo Peep . . .

Little Bo Peep
has lost her sheep –

Come
BAAAACK!

*Ahem!*
Little Bo Peep
has lost her sheep
and doesn't know where to find them –

**OH, DEAR!
Where have my darlings
run off to?**

. . .

**Beg your pardon.** I'm trying to recite a nursery rhyme here.

**My dear little lambs, always getting into jams!**

# AHEM!!!!

What's all that hullabaloo? Looks like those kittens need a talking to!

FINAL SALE!

BLACK SHEEP BROS.
ALL NATURAL WOOL

What a good boy am I!

Twee, tweedle dee, tweedle dee!

Twee, tweedle dee, tweedle dee!

★ JACK ★

# As I was saying,

Little Bo Peep
has lost her sheep
and doesn't know where to find them –

## HERE, BOY!

Lou, Lou, skip
to my Lou!

What
a great
fall!

Does **anybody** want to hear this nursery rhyme?

# WHERE, OH WHERE, HAS MY LITTLE DOG GONE?

Fly's in the buttermilk, shoo, fly, shoo.

*Seriously!* If you'll just listen!

I can't see
anything in this mess!
Going by foot may
be best.

# As I was TRYING to say,

Leave them alone,
and they'll come home,
wagging their tails behind them!

**OH, my SWEETS!**

**BAAAAAAD SHEEP!**

Little Bo Peep
has lost her sheep
and doesn't know where to find them.
Leave them alone,
and they'll come home,
wagging their tails behind them.

*(My sincerest apologies for the interruptions.*
*How could I get a word in with all that hullabaloo?)*

BUZZ
**BUZZ**
BUZZ

# DID YOU SPOT THE CHARACTERS FROM THESE CLASSIC NURSERY RHYMES?

## Little Bo Peep

Little Bo Peep
has lost her sheep
and doesn't know where
to find them.
Leave them alone,
and they'll come home,
wagging their tails
behind them.

## Do You Know the Muffin Man?

Do you know the Muffin Man,
the Muffin Man,
the Muffin Man?
Do you know the Muffin Man
who lives in Drury Lane?

Yes, I know the Muffin Man,
the Muffin Man,
the Muffin Man.
Yes, I know the Muffin Man
who lives in Drury Lane.

## Ring Around the Rosie

(also called Ring-a-Ring O' Roses)

Ring-a-ring o' roses,
a pocket full of posies.
A-tishoo! A-tishoo!
We all fall down.

## Little Boy Blue

Little Boy Blue,
come blow your horn,
the sheep's in the meadow,
the cow's in the corn.
Where is that boy
who looks after the sheep?
Under the haystack
fast asleep.
Will you wake him?
Oh no, not I, for if I do
he will surely cry.

## Baa, Baa, Black Sheep

Baa, baa, black sheep,
have you any wool?
Yes, sir, yes, sir,
three bags full;
one for the master,
and one for the dame,
and one for the little boy
who lives down the lane.

## B-I-N-G-O

There was a farmer had a dog
and Bingo was his name-o.
B-I-N-G-O
B-I-N-G-O
B-I-N-G-O
And Bingo was his name-o.

## London Bridge

London Bridge is falling down,
falling down, falling down.
London Bridge is falling down,
my fair lady.

## Where Has My Little Dog Gone?

Where, oh where has
my little dog gone?
Oh where,
oh where can he be?
With his ears so short,
and his tail so long,
oh where,
oh where can he be?

## Three Little Kittens

Three little kittens,
they lost their mittens,
and they began to cry,
"Oh, mother dear, we sadly fear
our mittens we have lost."
"What! Lost your mittens,
you naughty kittens!
Then you shall have no pie."
"Mee-ow, mee-ow, mee-ow."
"Then you shall have no pie."

## There Was an Old Woman

There was an old woman
who lived in a shoe.
She had so many children,
she didn't know what to do.
She gave them some broth
without any bread,
then kissed them all soundly
and put them to bed.

## Hey, Diddle Diddle

Hey, diddle diddle,
the cat and the fiddle,
the cow jumped over the moon.
The little dog laughed,
to see such sport,
and the dish ran away
with the spoon.

## To Market, To Market

To market, to market,
to buy a fat pig.
Home again, home again,
jiggety-jig.
To market, to market,
to buy a fat hog.
Home again, home again,
jiggety-jog.

## There Was a Crooked Man

There was a crooked man,
and he walked a crooked mile.
He found a crooked sixpence
upon a crooked stile.
He bought a crooked cat,
which caught a crooked mouse,
and they all lived together
in a little crooked house.

## Little Jack Horner

Little Jack Horner
sat in the corner,
eating a Christmas pie.
He put in his thumb,
and pulled out a plum,
and said,
"What a good boy am I!"

## This Little Piggy

This little piggy went to market.
This little piggy stayed home.
This little piggy had roast beef.
This little piggy had none.
And this little piggy went,
"Whee whee whee!"
all the way home.

## Jack Be Nimble

Jack be nimble,
Jack be quick,
Jack jump over
the candlestick.

## Skip to My Lou

Lou, Lou, skip to my Lou!
Lou, Lou, skip to my Lou!
Lou, Lou, skip to my Lou!
Skip to my Lou, my darling!

Fly's in the buttermilk, shoo, fly, shoo!
Fly's in the buttermilk, shoo, fly, shoo!
Fly's in the buttermilk, shoo, fly, shoo!
Skip to my Lou, my darling!

Lost my partner, what'll I do?
Lost my partner, what'll I do?
Lost my partner, what'll I do?
Skip to my Lou, my darling!

## The Itsy Bitsy Spider

The itsy bitsy spider
went up the waterspout.
Down came the rain
and washed the spider out.
Out came the sun
and dried up all the rain,
and the itsy bitsy spider
went up the spout again.

## Pat-a-Cake

Pat-a-cake, pat-a-cake,
baker's man.
Bake me a cake
as fast as you can.
Pat it and shape it
and mark it with "B".
And put it in the oven
for baby and me.

## Humpty Dumpty

Humpty Dumpty
sat on a wall.
Humpty Dumpty
had a great fall.
All the king's horses
and all the king's men
couldn't put Humpty
together again.

## Mary Had a Little Lamb

Mary had a little lamb,
its fleece was white as snow,
and everywhere
that Mary went,
the lamb was sure to go.

## Georgie Porgie

Georgie Porgie,
puddin' and pie,
kissed the girls
and made them cry.
When the boys
came out to play
Georgie Porgie
ran away.

## Little Miss Muffet

Little Miss Muffet
sat on a tuffet,
eating her curds
and whey.
Along came a spider,
who sat down beside her,
and frightened
Miss Muffet away.

## Pease Porridge Hot

Pease porridge hot,
pease porridge cold,
pease porridge in the pot,
nine days old.
Some like it hot,
some like it cold,
some like it in the pot,
nine days old.

## Mary, Mary, Quite Contrary

Mary, Mary, quite contrary,
how does your garden grow?
With silver bells and cockle shells,
and pretty maids all in a row.

## Jack and Jill

Jack and Jill
went up the hill
to fetch a pail of water.
Jack fell down
and broke his crown,
and Jill came tumbling after.

## Little Robin Redbreast

Little Robin Redbreast
sat upon a tree.
Up went the Pussy Cat,
and down went he.
Down came Pussy Cat,
away Robin ran.
Says little Robin Redbreast,
"Catch me if you can!"

## Wee Willie Winkie

Wee Willie Winkie
runs through the town,
upstairs and downstairs
in his nightgown.
Rapping at the window,
crying at the lock,
"Are the children
in their beds,
for now it's eight o'clock?"

## Rub-A-Dub-Dub

Rub-a-dub-dub,
three men in a tub,
and who do you think
they were?
The butcher, the baker,
the candlestick maker,
and all of them gone
to the fair!

For my three bears,
You are my greatest adventure. – A.L.W.

# A.L. Wegwerth

A.L. Wegwerth has an uncanny ability to recall songs and rhymes from childhood with little-to-no prodding. As one might imagine, this remarkable skill comes in handy on a daily basis – or at least for the time it took to create this book. She lives in Minnesota, USA with her husband and kids.

# Luke Flowers

Luke Flowers is an illuminator of the imagination from Colorado, USA where he lives with his wife and three kids. When he is not illustrating and writing children's books in his cosy creative cave, he finds deep inspiration in strumming on his guitar or banjo, going on adventures with his family, and savouring a unique blend of music, movies, coffee, and books . . . lots and lots of books.

**LITTLE BO PEEP AND HER BAD, BAD SHEEP © 2016 BY CURIOUS FOX.**

First published in 2016 by Curious Fox, an imprint of Capstone Global Library Limited, 264 Banbury Road, Oxford, OX2 7DY
Registered company number: 6695582
www.curious-fox.com
The author's moral rights are hereby asserted.
Illustrations by Luke Flowers
All characters in this publication are fictitious and any resemblance to real persons, living or dead, is purely coincidental.
ISBN 978-1-78202-366-1
19 18 17 16 15
10 9 8 7 6 5 4 3 2 1
A CIP catalogue for this book is available from the British Library.

Printed and bound in China.